Lewis and Clark

Kathleen E. Bradley

Associate Editor
Torrey Maloof

Editor
Wendy Conklin, M.A.

Editorial Director
Dona Herweck Rice

Editor-in-Chief
Sharon Coan, M.S.Ed.

Editorial Manager
Gisela Lee, M.A.

Creative Director
Lee Aucoin

Illustration Manager/Designer
Timothy J. Bradley

Cover Designer
Lesley Palmer

Cover Art
The Granger Collection, New York
The Library of Congress

Publisher
Rachelle Cracchiolo, M.S.Ed.

Teacher Created Materials
5301 Oceanus Drive
Huntington Beach, CA 92649
http://www.tcmpub.com
ISBN 978-1-4333-0540-5
© 2010 Teacher Created Materials, Inc.
Reprinted 2013

Lewis and Clark

Story Summary

This reader's theater is about the adventures of Lewis and Clark. They are the two co-captains of the Corps of Discovery. They have been sent on a mission by President Jefferson to find a water route from the Rocky Mountains to the Pacific Ocean. The Corps faces much danger and many obstacles during its journey west. Sacagawea, a Shoshone Indian, serves as a translator and a guide on the expedition. She helps the Corps find a group of Shoshone Indians. The Indians provide Lewis and Clark with horses to carry their supplies over the Rocky Mountains. With the help of the Shoshone Indians, Lewis and Clark are able to continue on their mission.

Tips for Performing
Reader's Theater

Adapted from Aaron Shepard

- Don't let your script hide your face. If you can't see the audience, your script is too high.

- Look up often when you speak. Don't just look at your script.

- Talk slowly so the audience knows what you are saying.

- Talk loudly so everyone can hear you.

- Talk with feelings. If the character is sad, let your voice be sad. If the character is surprised, let your voice be surprised.

- Stand up straight. Keep your hands and feet still.

- Remember that even when you are not talking, you are still your character.

Tips for Performing
Reader's Theater *(cont.)*

- If the audience laughs, wait for them to stop before you speak again.

- If someone in the audience talks, don't pay attention.

- If someone walks into the room, don't pay attention.

- If you make a mistake, pretend it was right.

- If you drop something, try to leave it where it is until the audience is looking somewhere else.

- If a reader forgets to read his or her part, see if you can read the part instead, make something up, or just skip over it. Don't whisper to the reader!

Lewis and Clark

Characters

George Drouillard	Sacagawea
Meriwether Lewis	Scout
William Clark	Chief Cameahwait

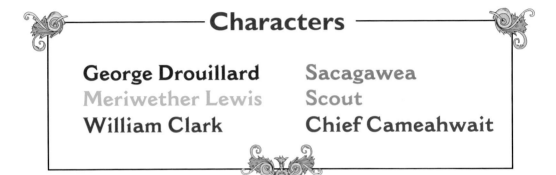

Setting

The story begins in 1805. The **Corps of Discovery** is traveling by canoe along the **Jefferson River**. It is about to reach the **Rocky Mountains**. The Corps splits into two groups to try and find the **Shoshone Indians**. One group travels on foot while the other group continues upstream in canoes. The two groups reunite at **Camp Fortunate**. They then travel to the Shoshone Indians' camp at the foot of the Rocky Mountains.

Act I

Drouillard: It has been days since we entered the Jefferson River. We need to move forward. We need to cross the mountains.

Lewis: Sacagawea, where are the Shoshone Indians? We need to barter some of our goods for their fine horses. The horses can help us carry our supplies across the mountains.

Sacagawea: Each year, my people come to live in this area. They come between the summer and the fall moons to catch the salmon from the river and pick the berries that grow along the riverbank.

Clark: Sacagawea, you were just a child the last time you were in this area. Perhaps you have forgotten what the area looks like.

Sacagawea: No, I have not forgotten. Five summers ago, the Minnetares Indians raided our tribe and stole our horses. They also stole the lives of many of my people, including my mother. I will remember the place when I see it.

Lewis: Winter will come early, and if we do not find your people soon, our expedition will need to be delayed, even canceled. The crew may not be able to survive a winter here.

Sacagawea: Captain Lewis, I assure you, we will not need to cancel the expedition. We will find the Shoshones soon enough. Once we do, I have no doubt that they will help us in any way they can.

Clark: It has been months since we last saw a single tribe. Since this land is uncharted, we have no maps to guide us in the right direction. Sacagawea, you are our only hope.

Sacagawea: I understand your concern, but I feel that we are very close. Great Spirit is guiding me. I am looking for a special landmark. This landmark will help us find the Shoshones.

Drouillard: Our food supply is very low. Soon we will have to make a decision concerning the fate of our mission. But for now, let's keep moving upriver. After breakfast, I will get the crews, supplies, and canoes ready to leave. Sacagawea, go get your husband and son. I believe I last saw them north of the river bend, just past that clearing.

Sacagawea: There it is! Private Drouillard, you have found it! The spot to which you are pointing is exactly the landmark I was trying so hard to find. That is Beaverhead Rock, and the area northwest of that rock is where you will find my people.

Poem: Sacagawea's Song

Act 2

Drouillard: Breakfast is ready! There is more than enough roasted beaver tail, grits, and red chokeberries to go around. Everyone, come eat! We have a long day ahead of us. Here, Captain Lewis, take this plate.

Lewis: Thank you, Private Drouillard.

Drouillard: Captain Lewis, I believe it would be best if we divided the crew into two groups. A few of us can go ahead and search this new area on foot. The others can continue upstream in the canoes.

Lewis: That is a great plan. You and I will travel on foot with two other privates. We will be able to track the Shoshones, and I can look for new plants and animals along the way.

Sacagawea: Captain, take this blanket with you. When greeting my people, you must use a blanket to signal that you come in friendship.

Lewis: I understand.

Sacagawea: Many tribes visit this area for the summer. The Shoshones do not have many weapons. They mainly have bows and arrows, whereas the other tribes have firearms. Because of this, they will be on the defense.

Lewis: Thank you for this valuable insight. I do not want to lose the chance to negotiate with your people when we so desperately need their help.

Clark: Good luck, Captain Lewis. I have a good feeling about this. You are the best man for tracking on foot. These last few months, you have discovered a variety of new plant and animal species never before seen by the white man. So, I suspect you will have absolutely no trouble locating the Shoshone Indians.

Sacagawea: They will most likely be fishing. They will be trying to catch the last of the salmon. And they will be gathering berries. Look for their footprints along the river.

Clark: Keep your looking glass ready, Captain Lewis. I am certain you will find the Shoshones before we do. With a smaller search party, the timid Shoshones may not feel as threatened and may be more willing to meet with you.

Act 3

Lewis: Private Drouillard, look there! Do you see the Indian about two miles straight ahead of us? He's up on the ridge, and it looks as if he is riding bareback upon his horse. I'll bet he's a Shoshone. I must send the blanket signal.

Scout: Chief Cameahwait and his braves will be going away soon to hunt the bison, and he wants to be sure that the women and children will be safe from enemy tribal raids while he is gone. Who are these men, and what are they looking for?

Drouillard: It looks as if he is approaching, but cautiously.

Scout: This is not a good time for strangers to emerge. Why are they fully dressed at this time of year? There hasn't even been a snow yet. Oh, no! They are carrying firearms! I must hurry and warn the chief at once.

Lewis: Oh, no! He's retreating!

Drouillard: He has leapt onto his horse and is headed straight for the willow brush. We must not lose him! We can follow him to his tribe if we hurry!

Lewis: Look! The horse tracks lead in this direction, so we must be getting close. The Shoshone camp is probably just west of here.

Drouillard: Captain Lewis, wait! Look over there to the northeast! There are three Indian women standing by the riverbank. Perhaps we can persuade them to take us to their chief.

Lewis: I will go speak with the women. You three men stay here, and I will return in a moment.

Drouillard: Good luck, Captain Lewis.

Cameahwait: Warriors! Advance!

Drouillard: Oh, no! The Indian we saw earlier must have alerted his tribe because there are at least 60 warriors on horses coming this way at full speed! Captain Lewis, look out!

Cameahwait: Warriors! Stop! Obey your chief's command. There are women from our tribe in the vicinity. We will proceed with caution. Strangers to this land, state your purpose at once.

Lewis: My men and I come in peace. My name is Captain Lewis. I place my rifle to the ground and step before you unarmed. Are you of the Shoshone tribe?

Scout: We are. Chief Cameahwait, these are the men I saw. They were combing the area along the riverbank. They are looking for something.

Cameahwait: Strangers, what are you searching for?

Lewis: You! We were looking for you and your tribe.

Drouillard: Our leader, President Jefferson, has sent us on a journey of discovery. We wish to barter for some of your fine horses so that we can cross the mountains behind you.

Cameahwait: We are preparing to leave for our summer bison hunt. There is no time to barter.

Scout: They could be scouts for the Pahkee. If this is the case, then our people are in great danger.

Cameahwait: No. A man who lays down his weapons before us poses no threat.

Lewis: We lay down our firearms and give to you our country's flag. It is the greatest symbol of our honesty and friendship.

Cameahwait: Why is your skin white? To what tribe do you belong?

Lewis: We are not of any Indian tribe. We are white men.

Scout: We have heard of men with white skin, but we have never seen one.

Drouillard: Our leader wishes us to find a direct route to the ocean on the other side of those mountains. Do you know of a body of water that stretches to where the sun sets?

Cameahwait: The Shoshones do not venture beyond those mountains. However, we do barter with tribes that sometimes trade shells for our horses. See what I wear around my neck? I was told this shell that hangs in the center of these bear claws is from the great ocean you seek.

Scout: It is incredibly dangerous to travel without firearms. Besides, why hunt in the rugged mountain terrain when there is nothing to eat there? It is only on the plains that we find bison. What is it you need from us, and how do we know we can trust you?

Lewis: You do not know, but we know that we can trust you. A Shoshone woman travels with us. As a girl, she was taken captive by the Minnetares and then traded to one of the interpreters we hired for this journey. She has said that your tribe can be trusted.

Cameahwait: Where is this mystery woman?

Drouillard: She is with a second group of our people. They are traveling by canoes to transport all of our supplies. They will be here soon.

Scout: There is only one thing our tribe needs, and that is firearms. Did she mention how desperately we are in need of firearms for protection?

Drouillard: Yes. She was very clear about that point.

Cameahwait: The enemy tribes, like the Minnetares and Blackfeet, have firearms. They have raided our camp many times. We need firearms to protect and feed our families.

Scout: It is very difficult to hunt bison with a bow and arrow. The men from the other tribes are often stronger because they eat meat all year long. Meanwhile, we are forced to live like bears, surviving on fish, simple roots, and berries.

Lewis: Chief, I am sorry, but we did not bring extra firearms for bartering.

Drouillard: Can we barter today for a few of your horses without firearms as the price? If so, our leader will tell the white men that they may trade firearms with you in the future.

Scout: Chief Cameahwait, this white man speaks lies! His people are trying to take advantage of us.

Cameahwait: I disagree! With 60 warriors on horseback holding their bows and arrows, an untruthful man would have told me whatever I wished to hear. No, this man tells me the truth.

Lewis: Thank you for your trust.

Drouillard: We need your horses and your help to get across those mountains. If our journey is successful, your tribe will be considered a trusted and valuable bartering partner and your wish for firearms will be realized. We give you our word.

Act 4

Cameahwait: You said that the rest of your party would be here soon and would be ready to barter. We are extremely disappointed.

Scout: We delayed our bison hunt by three days and have walked many miles away from the hunt. Everyone believes we are being led into a trap. I have a feeling this was a horrible mistake! We should have never trusted these white men.

Drouillard: Nonsense! Take our rifles, and if you feel threatened before the sun rises, use them. However, I tell you our people are coming.

Lewis: Private Drouillard, tomorrow you will leave here and go find Captain Clark. I'm sure he is late because the river is so treacherous.

Scout: Maybe it is Great Spirit's feeling that this land is not for white men. Chief Cameahwait, I think we should return to the hunt right now.

Drouillard: Captain Lewis, look west about 40 paces! Captain Clark and the rest of the party have finally arrived! And just in time!

Clark: Oh! Captain Lewis, ol' friend! It sure is good to see you again! And you, too, Private Drouillard.

Drouillard: Captain Clark, what is Sacagawea doing? Why is she dancing with her fingertips to her mouth?

Scout: Through this woman's dance she is telling us that she is of our nation. She is one of us, and this is why my people are all shouting and rejoicing! They are happy to see one of their own return.

Sacagawea: He is right! They speak my language, and I recognize their dress and ways. This is a great sign. We have finally found the Shoshone! Thank you, Great Spirit!

Drouillard: Chief Cameahwait, you can now see, we are men of our words. Our party has arrived as promised. We have our goods here and are ready to barter with you.

Lewis: May we now begin the negotiations?

Sacagawea: The chief has laid down a white cloth for us to sit upon. It is an honor to do so and means he is ready to negotiate.

Clark: We, too, promise to barter fairly. The Shoshone people are known for their excellent horses. They are also wise regarding how to travel over this mountain range.

Cameahwait: I raise this sacred pipe first to the heavens. Then, I raise it in every direction that the wind blows across Great Spirit's land. We will each draw smoke from it to show our unity. It is Great Spirit's way that all who walk this earth live in harmony together.

Sacagawea: Chief, what is it about you that seems so familiar to me? Is it your choice of words? Is it your mannerisms?

Clark: Sacagawea, your eyes are filling with tears. What's wrong?

Sacagawea: Oh, nothing is wrong! Everything is absolutely perfect! These are not tears of sadness, but tears of pure joy. Chief, do you not recognize me? I am your sister! Our names and appearances have changed so much since we last saw one another. Five summers ago, you were but a boy, and I was just a young girl. Oh, brother, I have missed you terribly!

Cameahwait: Sister, it is you! I have hoped for a day such as this for so long. Now, after many moons, it has finally arrived.

Scout: I doubted these men at first, but now I believe Great Spirit has led them to us.

Sacagawea: Captains, Great Spirit did not lead you to just any Shoshone tribe—he led you to my tribe! Brother, please know that these men are honorable. Great Spirit guides them.

Clark: Private Drouillard, please play your fiddle! We shall all dance and enjoy this good fortune. We shall call this place Camp Fortunate.

Act 5

Cameahwait: I must protect my people from raiding enemy tribes. Other Indians see us as weak because we do not have firearms.

Scout: Once we have firearms, we will be able to defend ourselves. When word gets out, we will be left alone to live in peace.

Clark: During our journey, we have spoken with the Minnetares, Mandans, and Missouri tribes. They have promised to stop attacking the Shoshone.

Sacagawea: Captain Clark speaks the truth. I have been beside him during those meetings. These men mean no harm to the Shoshones. They want to help you retain firearms, but they need your help in return.

Scout: Ultimately, the firearms will be used to hunt so that our people will be well nourished, not to harm other human beings. Great Spirit has heard our prayers and is pleased with our request.

Clark: Then it is agreed! Trade between us and the Shoshone people will begin. With a direct route to the Pacific Ocean, just think of the goods we can barter with you.

Scout: My chief is disappointed that you cannot give us firearms now, but he is willing to wait.

Clark: Chief Cameahwait, please take this medal as a symbol of our commitment to your people. Owning it means that you are a friend of the United States government. On one side, it has a carving of the face of our leader, President Jefferson. On the back is a carving of two clasped hands next to a pipe and a tomahawk.

Cameahwait: I accept this medal with pride and honor. It will indeed be looked upon as a token of your commitment to my people.

Clark: We also offer you this uniform coat, shirt, tobacco, and a few other small articles. We hope these gifts will prove valuable to you and your tribe.

Cameahwait: The Shoshones will benefit from these gifts. For these items, I will trade you three of our horses. Now, I must leave and return to my tribe.

Scout: We are camped along the river at the foot of the mountains. We will return with horses to move your baggage from these canoes to our camp.

Cameahwait: Once you see that the mountains are impassable by water, we will negotiate further. We will provide you with fresh horses for your journey.

Clark: Agreed. Lewis, you stay here with our goods. I will go ahead with the chief, Sacagawea, and 11 of our men. While the chief is returning to you with more horses, we will explore the river to see if it can be navigated. If it can be, we will build canoes. Then, we will only need the Shoshones to help us bring our supplies to the new canoes. If the waterway is impassable, then we will negotiate for more horses.

Sacagawea: When we arrive at the camp, you should speak to an elderly Shoshone man. He is called Swooping Eagle, and he has ventured the farthest across the mountains. Isn't that right, Brother?

Cameahwait: Sister, you remember our people well. Swooping Eagle knows the fierce waterfalls and narrow trails that make up the mountains you wish to cross.

Clark: My compass can only keep us moving in the right direction. To have a Shoshone accompany us, one who knows the mountains well, would be a valuable asset. Can Swooping Eagle guide us?

Cameahwait: If Swooping Eagle wishes to help you for a price, it will be arranged.

Scout: We will leave for our camp as soon as the sun rises. I will introduce you to Swooping Eagle when we arrive. You can discuss taking him as your guide then.

Act 6

Drouillard: Captain Lewis, remember the three Shoshone women we encountered earlier?

Lewis: Of course! What about them? You seem upset, Private Drouillard. What is wrong?

Drouillard: We overheard them say that the chief has just instructed his people to pack up and move out of their camp. The very camp where we are planning to meet them to bargain for horses.

Lewis: This cannot be true! Sacagawea, find your chief at once! I must speak to him directly.

Sacagawea: What is wrong, Captain Lewis?

Clark: It looks as if your chief has betrayed us. He has broken his promise!

Sacagawea: I am sure there has been a misunderstanding. My brother is a man of his word and would not break his promise.

Clark: Captain Lewis, the chief is approaching.

Lewis: Chief Cameahwait, I thought you were a man of your word. You promised to assist us with our baggage to your camp. You promised to allow your people to negotiate with us for horses.

Cameahwait: These are all truths.

Clark: Then, Sir, why have you asked your people to leave their camp?

Cameahwait: Last night I received word that my people were hungry. The snow from the mountains will be down in the valleys within days, and I must get them food because the salmon are all gone.

Scout: The bison hunt cannot be delayed any longer.

Lewis: Everything we have promised, we have provided. Captain Clark arrived at Camp Fortunate. Gifts have been given to you. We even shared the kill our hunters obtained.

Scout: With their many firearms…

Clark: Enough! All you do is complain about firearms as if they are the only things that matter!

Scout: And all that you care about is crossing those mountains and finding the great ocean. You do not care if our people live or die. You just want to be able to tell your leader that your expedition was successful.

Clark: Chief Cameahwait, why can't you see that our crossing those mountains will in turn bring you firearms? Once we cross, trade will be established.

Cameahwait: You are correct. Let me send my scout back to the camp immediately. He will relay my order that my people are to remain until we arrive. I will make certain that you will be provided for in horses and in help.

Act 7

Lewis: I can see the Shoshone camp. The sun is setting on the buffalo-hide tepees, and I can see a bonfire and the Shoshone surrounding it.

Cameahwait: Please, Captain Lewis, sound your firearms just once. My scout has notified my people that you will announce your arrival by the sound of fire. This will be the first time that noise means good will and good fortune for my tribe.

Scout: Captain Lewis, you have arrived! My people will be happy to see you and will greet you and your crew warmly. I also have a written message from Captain Clark for you.

Lewis: My co-captain says that the waterways are indeed impassable and that we need more horses. Chief, may we barter with you once again for more of your fine horses?

Cameahwait: Of course! Captain Lewis, I would also like you to have this fur tippet made from the pelts of otters and one hundred white weasels. Please accept it as a reminder of the Shoshones and the promises that have been made between us.

Lewis: This is the most elegant piece of Indian dress I have ever seen. I am honored to accept it. The Shoshone people will be remembered fondly.

Sacagawea: We will dance and celebrate this happy occasion. We have much to be grateful for!

Lewis: Our journey will be a success!

Song: America the Beautiful

Sacagawea's Song

by Martha Hart-Johns

I am Sacagawea.
I am proud Sacagawea.
I am proud Shoshone.
Taken from my tribe as a child,
I have no parents.
The earth is my Mother, my teacher.
Sure of foot like the goat,
Stout of heart like the bear,
I grew to be a guide to men with pale faces.
On my journey I came upon my people wandering,
Like me, Proud Shoshone.
They greeted me and gave us horses.
Saved us and gave us horses.
Rocks and trees are my map.
For my children's children will say,
Proud Sacagawea, she led them across the land,
To the great crashing Western Water.
I will not be afraid.
Follow me.

This is an abridged version of the complete poem.

America the Beautiful

by Katherine Lee Bates

O beautiful for spacious skies,
For amber waves of grain,
For purple mountain majesties
Above the fruited plain!

Chorus:
America! America!
God shed His grace on thee,
And crown thy good with brotherhood
From sea to shining sea!

O beautiful for patriot dream
That sees beyond the years
Thine alabaster cities gleam
Undimmed by human tears.

Chorus

This is an abridged version of the complete song.

Glossary

alabaster—a smooth, usually white mineral used for carving

amber—a dark orange yellow

barter—trading for goods or services without the use of money

combing—searching carefully

expedition—a journey taken by a group of people for a specific purpose

firearms—rifles or handguns

gleam—a small visible light

looking glass—a telescope or mirror

majesties—a greatness of character

negotiate—to agree or compromise

spacious—large or vast in size and capacity

species—a class of the same kind of things with the same name

tippet—a scarf, shawl, or cape

treacherous—not safe because of hidden dangers

venture—to seek with an element of risk